HOW MONTY FOUND HIS MAGIC

First published 2017 by Walker Books Ltd, 87 Vauxhall Walk, London SE11 5HJ • 2 4 6 8 10 9 7 5 3 1 • © 2017 Lerryn Korda • The right of Lerryn Korda to be identified as author/illustrator of this work has been asserted by her in accordance with the Copyright, Designs and Patents Act 1988 • This book has been typeset in Futura Book • Printed in China • British Library Cataloguing in Publication Data: a catalogue record for this book is available from the British Library • ISBN 978-1-4063-5656-4 • www.walker.co.uk

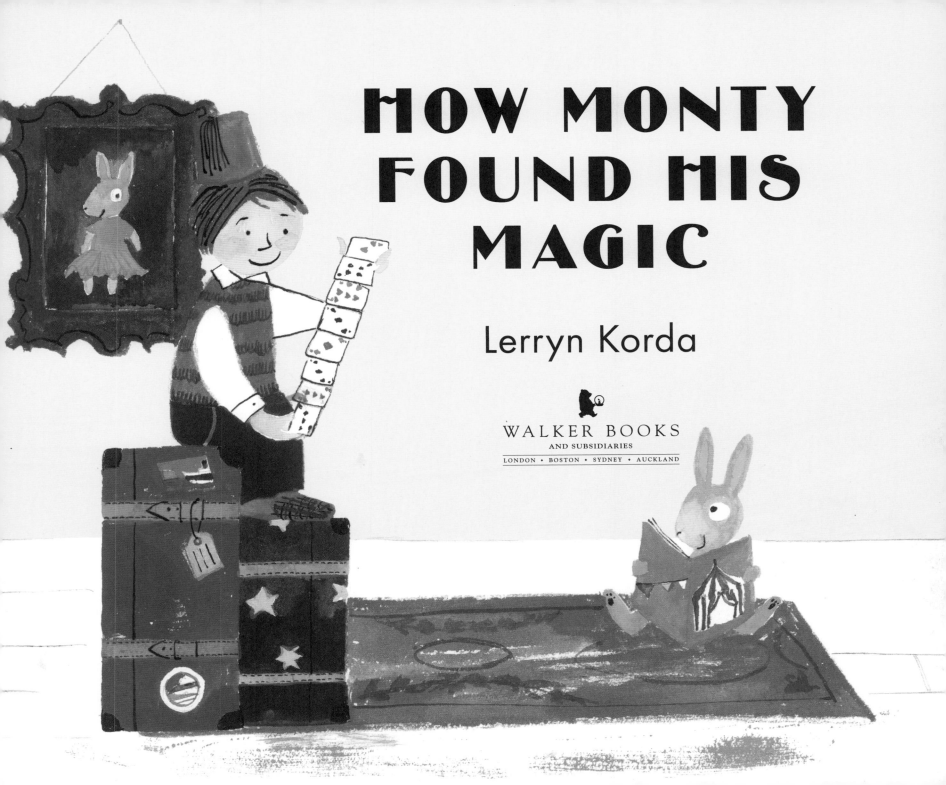

HOW MONTY FOUND HIS MAGIC

Lerryn Korda

WALKER BOOKS
AND SUBSIDIARIES
LONDON · BOSTON · SYDNEY · AUCKLAND

In quite a small house in a great big city lived three friends. A little boy called **Monty**, a rabbit called **Snuffles** ...

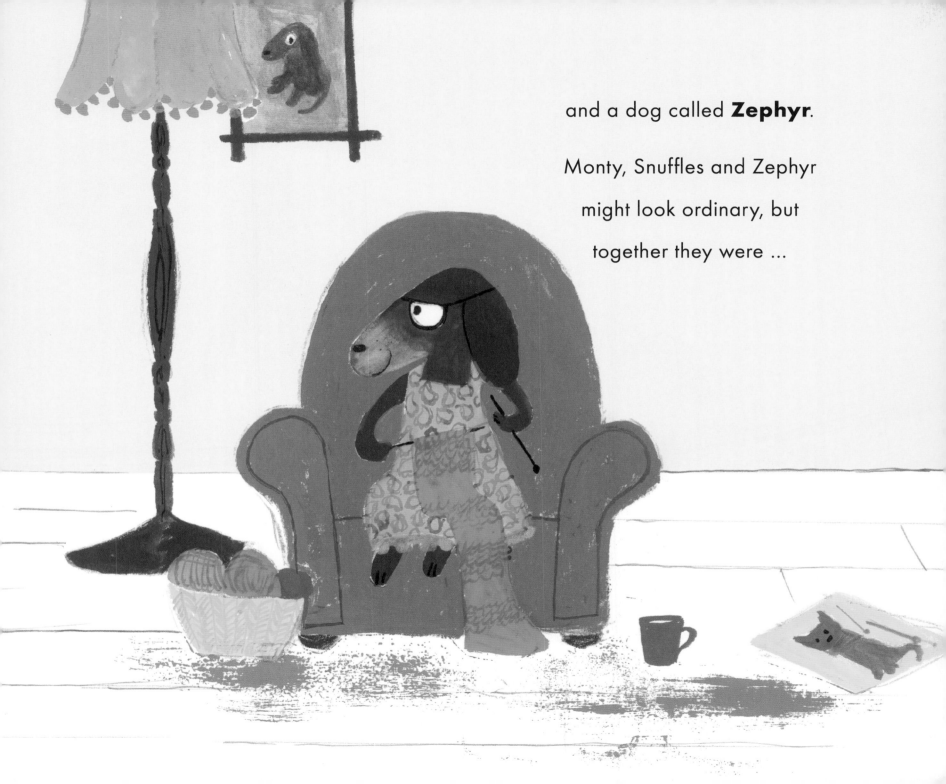

and a dog called **Zephyr**.

Monty, Snuffles and Zephyr
might look ordinary, but
together they were ...

The Magnificent Marvelloso Trio!

They dazzled with their
Hair-Raising Hat Trick,

they razzled with their
Snake-Charming String Trick,
and they whirled and they twirled
and they shimmied and they swirled
before doing their Supernatural
Sawing-in-Half Trick ...

and they dreamed of
razzling and dazzling a
real audience one day.

The only problem was that whenever Monty tried to perform a magic trick in the outside world, he got so many butterflies in his tummy, he just couldn't do it.

Zephyr wished he knew how to help Monty feel marvellously magical all the time.

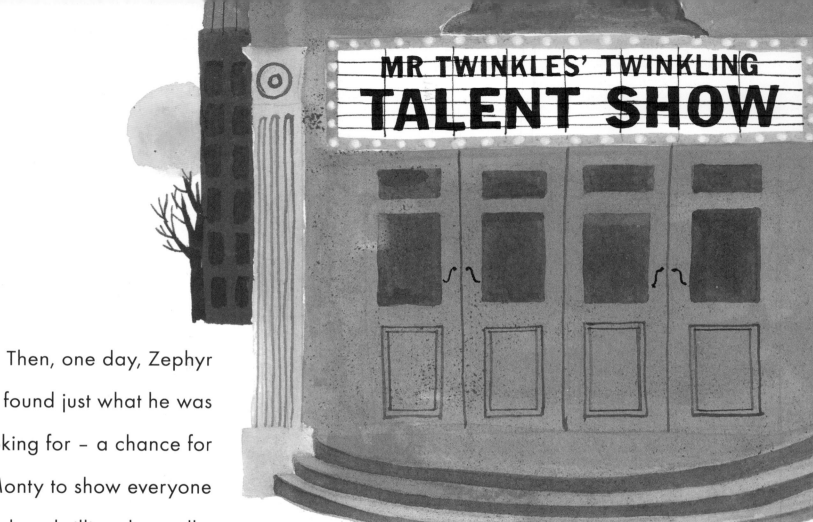

MR TWINKLES' TWINKLING
TALENT SHOW

Then, one day, Zephyr
found just what he was
looking for – a chance for
Monty to show everyone
how brilliant he really was.

But Monty was not so sure.

"Don't worry," said Zephyr.
"We'll be **together**."

When they were home,

Zephyr and Snuffles got on the phone.

The very next day an important letter arrived in the post:

TWINKLES

MY DEAR MAGNIFICENT
MARVELLOSO TRIO!

I invite you to conjure your most magical
tricks in front of the grandest gathering
this great big city has ever seen!

Yours, in anticipation, always

Mr Twinkles

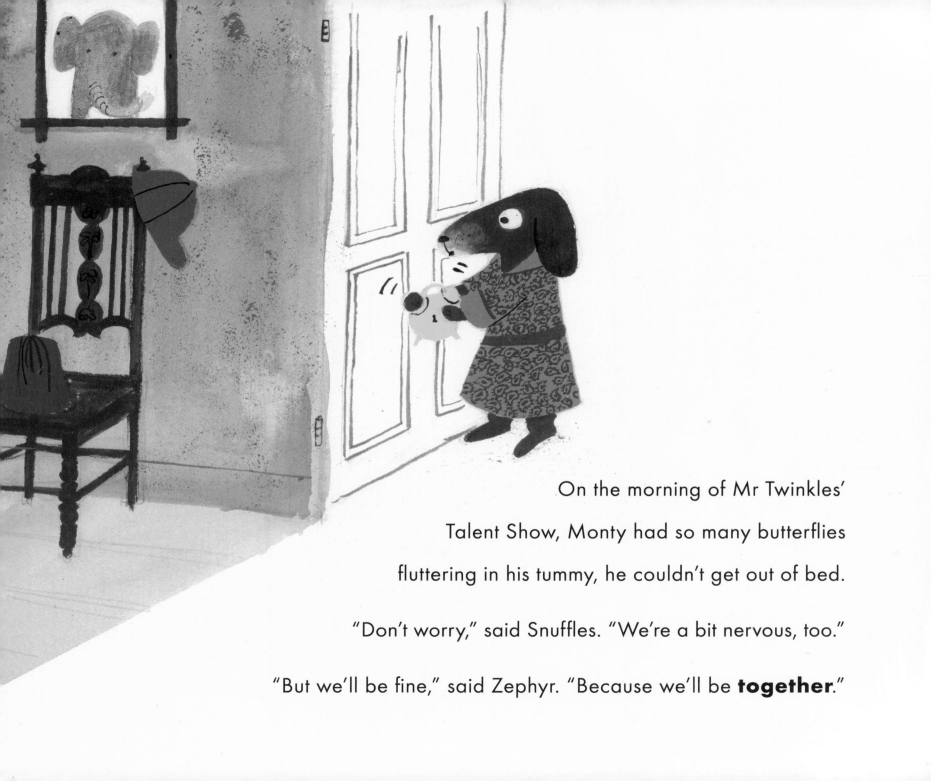

On the morning of Mr Twinkles'
Talent Show, Monty had so many butterflies
fluttering in his tummy, he couldn't get out of bed.

"Don't worry," said Snuffles. "We're a bit nervous, too."

"But we'll be fine," said Zephyr. "Because we'll be **together**."

Zephyr and Snuffles made a special breakfast bursting with all their favourite magical combinations!

Monty tried on lots of silly costumes until he found one that was just right.

Then they got
to Mr Twinkles'
Talent Show just
about on time...

It was Monty and Snuffles
and Zephyr's turn to go on stage.

There were so many talented poodles
and pirouetting pandas, the butterflies in Monty's
tummy fluttered faster than ever.

Then Mr Twinkles called out, "Ladies and
gentlemen, please put your hands together for …"

"The Magnificent Marvelloso Trio!"

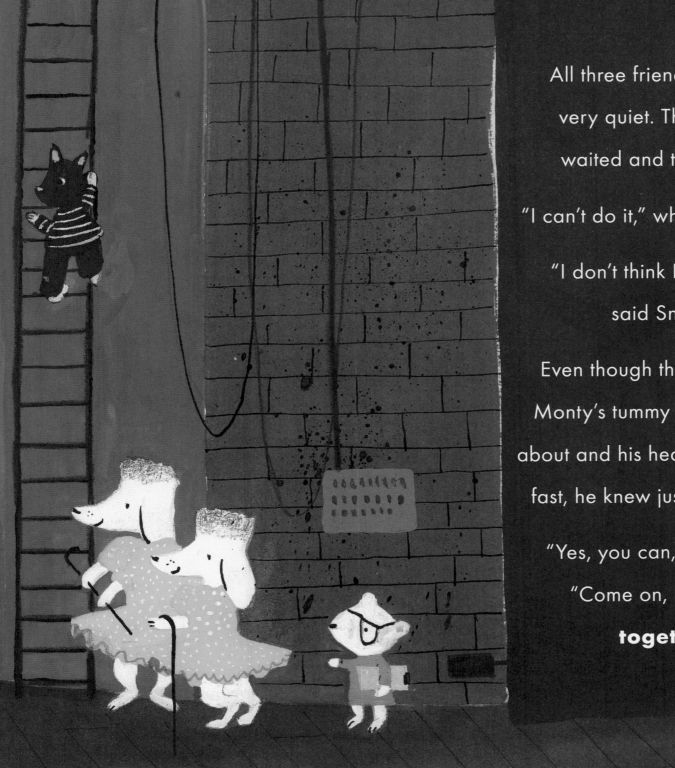

All three friends went very, very quiet. The audience waited and they waited.

"I can't do it," whispered Zephyr.

"I don't think I can, either," said Snuffles.

Even though the butterflies in Monty's tummy were whizzing about and his heart was thumping fast, he knew just what to say...

"Yes, you can," said Monty. "Come on, let's do this **together**."

Monty and Snuffles
and Zephyr conjured
up all their courage
and marched out
onto the stage.

Together they performed their Hair-Raising Hat Trick, their Snake-Charming String Trick, and they whirled and they twirled and they shimmied and they swirled before doing their Supernatural Sawing-in-Half Trick!

Then the moment came for ...

ABRACADABRA ABRACA—

BOOOM!

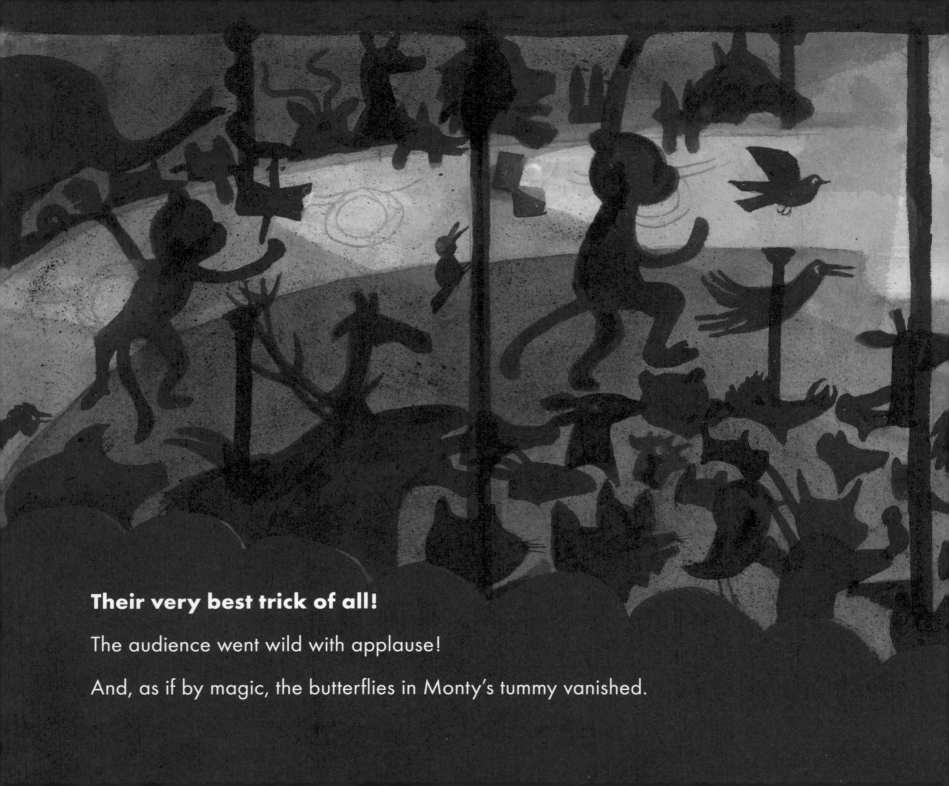

Their very best trick of all!

The audience went wild with applause!

And, as if by magic, the butterflies in Monty's tummy vanished.

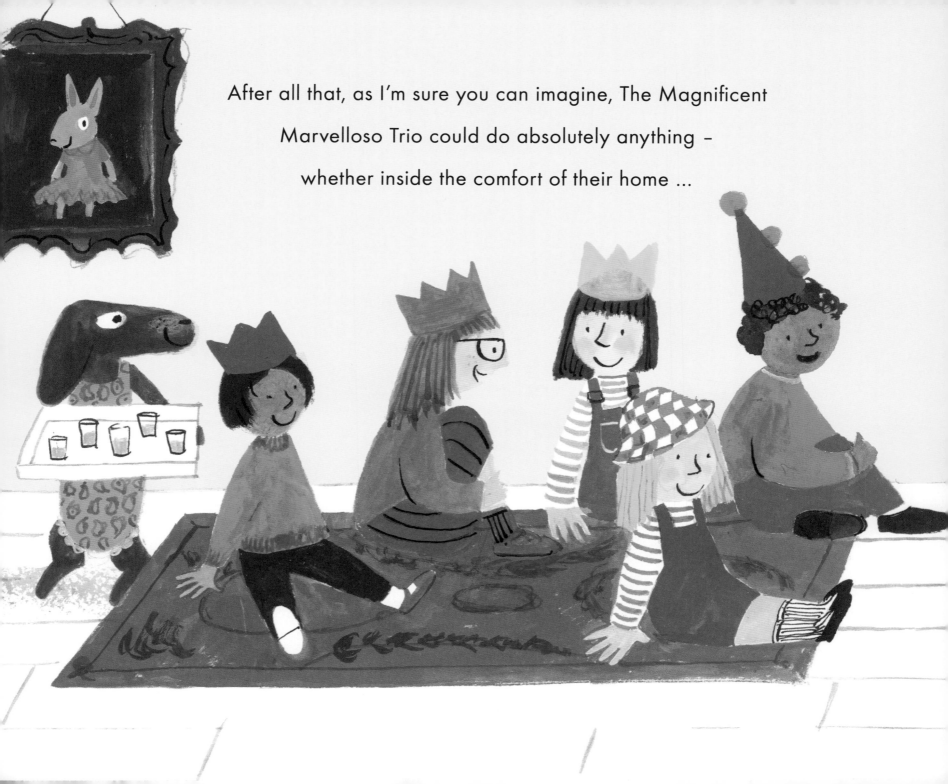

After all that, as I'm sure you can imagine, The Magnificent Marvelloso Trio could do absolutely anything – whether inside the comfort of their home ...

or outside in the big wide world ...

just as long as they were **together**.